Bugs in my Hair!

David Shannon

The Blue Sky Press • An Imprint of Scholastic Inc. • New York

To moms everywhere
and their battle-tested anti-lice weapons

This book was originally published in hardcover by The Blue Sky Press in 2013.

ISBN 978-0-545-78858-8

12 11 10 9 8 7 6 5 4 3 2 1   14 15 16 17 18 19/0

Printed in the U.S.A.   88

First Scholastic paperback printing, September 2014

One day, my mom made a terrible, awful discovery...

HEAD LICE!

There were
BUGS!!
In my
HAIR!!
And they were laying
EGGS*!!

* Lice eggs are called "nits."

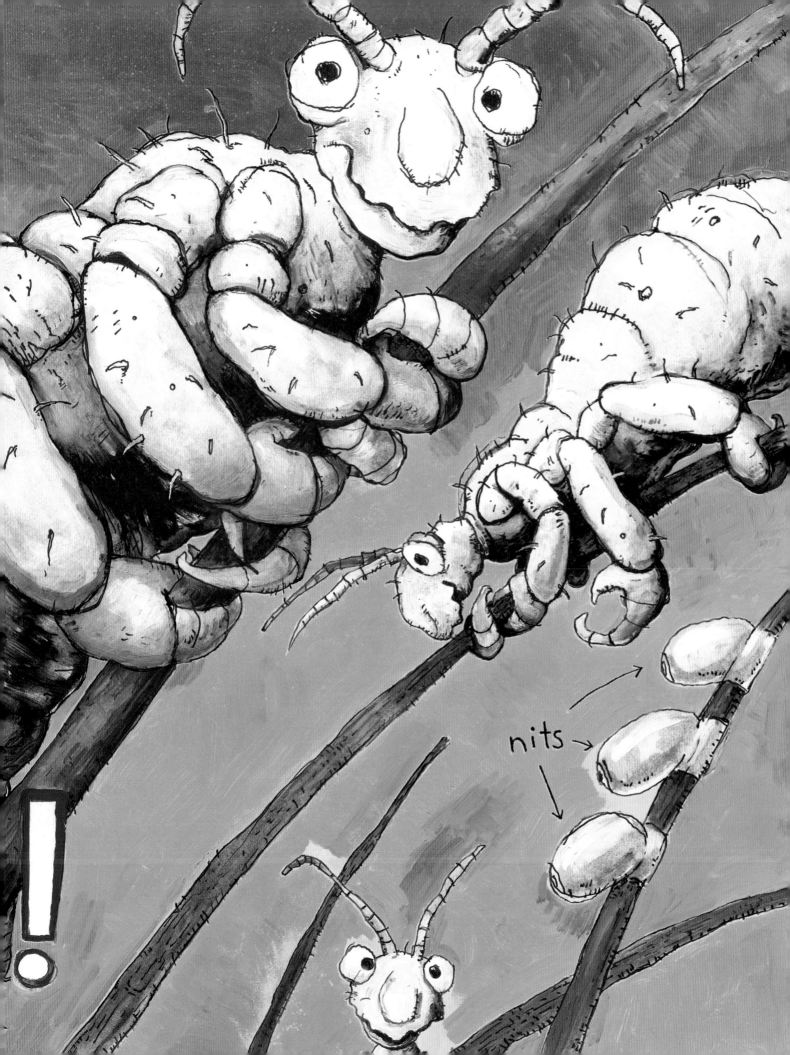

nits

Actually, they were feasting on my BLOOD.*

*Ick!

Oh, the SHAME

The Humiliation!

Everyone will know.
I won't have any frie

It was hard for some to admit they had lice (even to themselves.

"That's just dandruff."

"I think it's sand from the beach."

"It's probably ash from that volcano in Pogo Pogo."

Other people thought they had lice even when they didn't. Just talking about bugs made my mom itchy. Her problem wasn't _on_ her head, it was _in_ her head!

I heard about

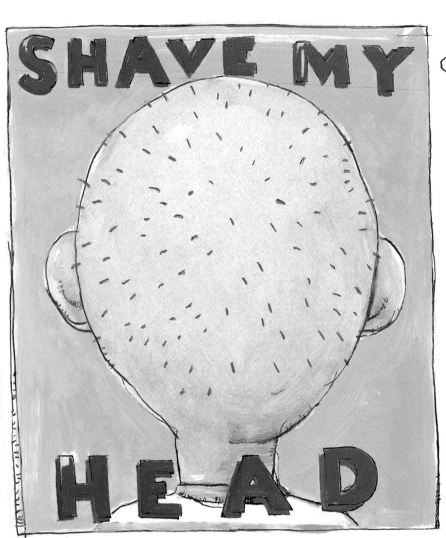

SHAVE MY HEAD

BOMB the BUGS with the strongest chemicals known to mankind.

They all sou

lots of cures.

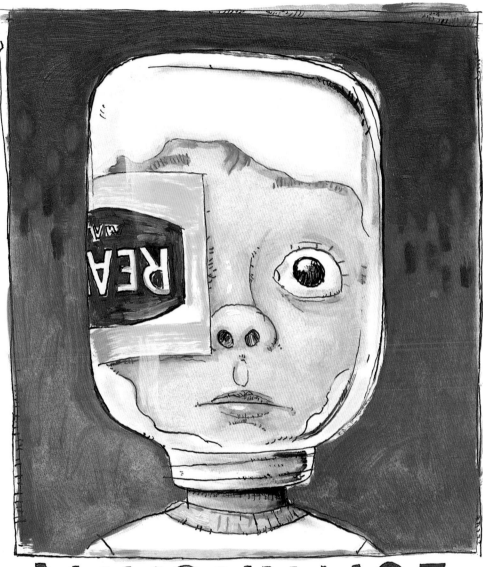

MAYONNAISE

nded AWFUL!

Lice are really hard to get rid of.

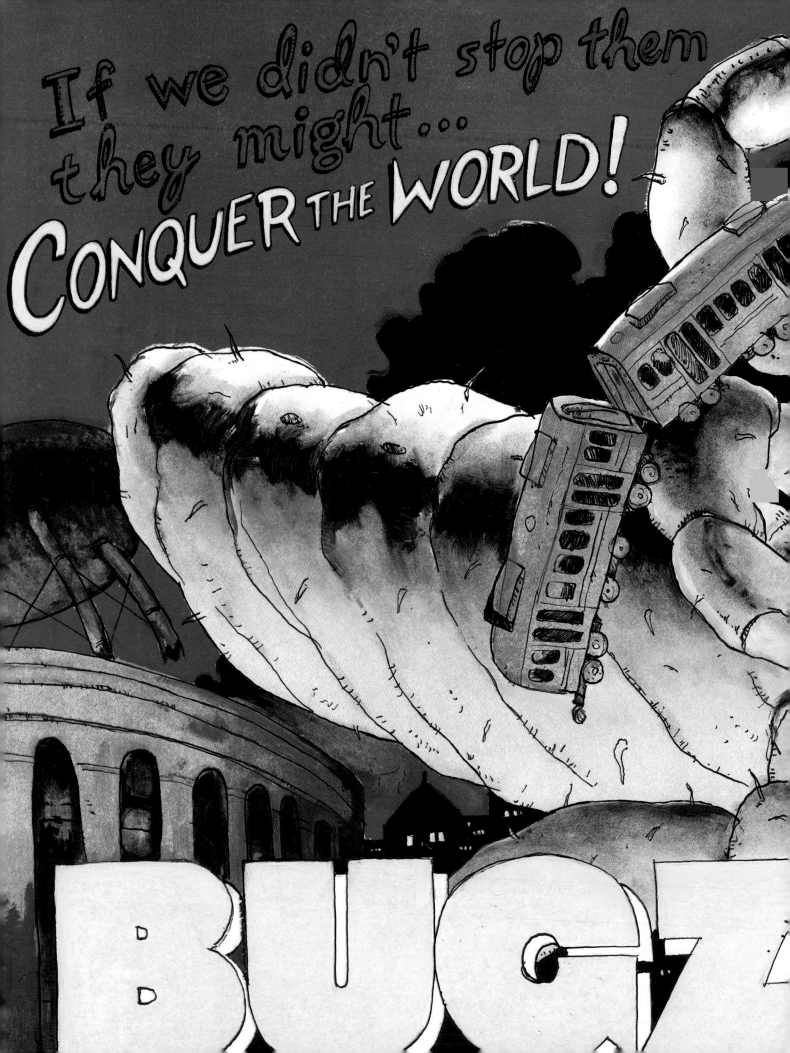

Nit comb →

Mom read lots of books and magazines and she armed herself with battle-tested anti-lice weapons.

Finally, everything was laundered, treated, sprayed, combed, picked,* and cleaned. We went to a professional lice treatment place and I was pronounced bug-free!

* Guess where we get the term "nitpicking."

For the first time in forever
I got a good night's sleep.

And then...

So we went through the whole thing again and now, at last, those awful, disgusting lice are completely gone. And this time...

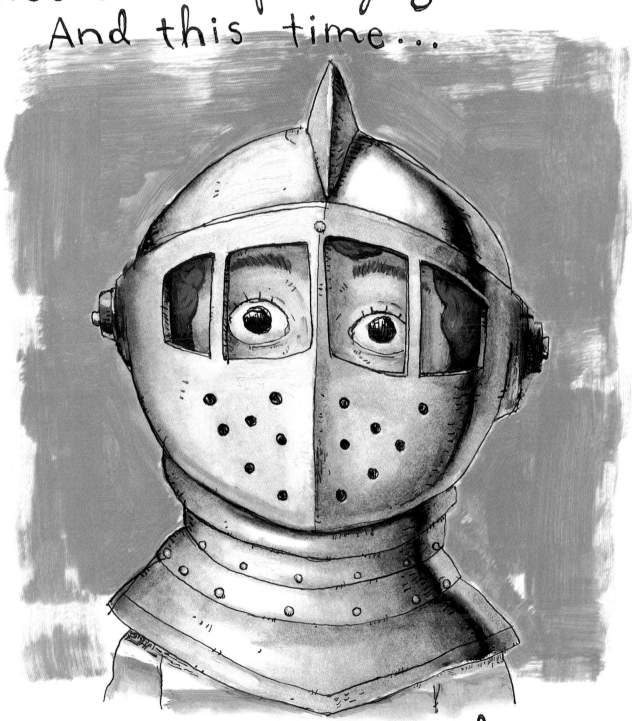

I'm not taking any chances!